I0537946

White Christmas

A Paranormal Romantic Suspense Novella

By Rebecca York

Ruth Glick writing as Rebecca York

Published by Light Street Press
Copyright © 2016 by Ruth Glick
Cover design by Earthly Charms

ISBN: 978-1943191055.

CHAPTER ONE

Amelia Parsons was too upset to see the car speeding toward her through the swirling snow. One moment she was crossing an ice-rutted street in St. Stephens, Maryland, and worrying about a call from the FBI—plus a missing shipment of Christmas ornaments for the hospital tree. In the next she was flying into the air. She heard someone scream. Maybe it was her. Then she sank into thick blackness that lasted for minutes—or maybe it was years.

When her eyes blinked open, she was standing in the cold again, wavering on unsteady legs as big flakes came down around her like she was the star attraction in a giant snow globe.

Main Street was gone. Instead, in her blurry vision, she saw pine trees, their branches weighted down with a layer of ice.

Her head hurt and her mind felt muzzy. She thought she heard holiday music drifting toward her on the wind—maybe White Christmas. Or was it only ringing in her ears? And were the lights in the distance real? Through the falling snow and the trees, she could just make them out.

She'd been downtown, half a block from The Wild Side, her arts and crafts shop which sold the work of local artisans as well as native crafts from around the world. Now somehow she was out in the woods, but the lights must mean she wasn't far from civilization.

The snow on the ground was almost over the top of her boots. As she struggled toward the vague outline of several oversized Swiss chalets, she tripped against a root, going down on her hands and knees.

For a few moments, she fought a pitched battle to keep from blacking out again. When her vision cleared, she pushed herself up and had to grab the trunk of a tree for support.

"Get it together, Amelia," she muttered as she started struggling toward the lights again.

Before she had gotten more than a few yards, she heard an ominous rumbling that seemed to be coming from high up and to her left. It thundered closer, and the image of an avalanche hurtling down the side of a mountain leaped into her fogged mind.

All she could do was scramble for safety, floundering through the drifts like a seal out of water, trying to reach the building ahead. A torrent of white enveloped her, and she knew she wasn't going to make it. Just before she went under, a running figure grabbed her, swooping her up in strong arms.

She had a quick impression of dark hair under a fur-trimmed hood, fierce eyes, and a clenched jaw as he ran with her, lumps of ice pelting down on both of them. He must have zoomed out of the main mass of the avalanche because she sensed it rumbling behind them as he kept going, heading for the closest building.

After he crossed the threshold and carried her inside, she realized they were in a barn where animals were making snorting and chattering sounds. But when she peered into a couple of stalls, there were no cows or horses. Instead she saw beige- and brown-colored beasts with antlers. They looked like some kind of deer. But who kept deer in a stable?

Strange as it seemed, she would have sworn they were talking excitedly to each other, or was that just the ringing in her ears? At any rate, she couldn't understand what they were saying. And before she could figure it out, her rescuer took her to an unused stall and set her down while he threw back his hood and brushed snow off his shoulders.

Unsteady on her feet, she backed up and landed in a large pile of hay.

Now that they were out of danger, she could get a better look at the guy towering over her. He was a hunk wearing jeans, a dark coat and heavy gloves. Under other circumstances, she might have tried to get friendly, but his icy eyes stopped her.

"Thank you for saving me," she tried as a kind of, um, icebreaker. When he didn't reply, she kept talking. "I mean, I know I put you in jeopardy. I'm sorry."

His answer wasn't what she'd expected. "What are you doing here?"

Her clouded brain struggled to process the question. "I don't know. I mean I don't even know where I am."

He glared down at her. "I think you know all right. Who sent you?"

"Nobody."

As she spoke, she heard footsteps in the corridor between the stalls. A short, plump man dressed in jeans

3

and a red coat over a red flannel shirt stepped into the stall. His thick white hair was mussed, and his bushy white beard hid the bottom half of his face.

"What's going on?" he asked.

"I found her out in the snow. I think she's a spy."

Amelia stared at him in disbelief. "A spy? I don't even know where I am," she repeated what she'd said earlier, then added, "My name is Amelia Parsons. I own a craft shop in St Stephens, Maryland. I was minding my own business when ..." She stopped and pressed her fingers to her mouth. "Oh Lord, I think I was hit by a car. I was so upset about that call from the FBI—plus the Santa's Workshop shipping delay."

They both stared at her. "What do you know about the problems at Santa's Workshop?" the hunk demanded.

Again she struggled for coherent thoughts. "Nothing. I was supposed to get a discount order of ornaments, for the hospital tree, but the distributor can't get anything from them."

The men exchanged glances.

When the older one started to speak, the younger guy shook his head. "Need-to-know basis."

Amelia blinked. "Huh?"

The bearded man turned back to Amelia. "We've had some problems lately. I guess I should be more cautious, but it's hard not to expect the best from people."

"Would you mind telling me your names?" she asked, her gaze swinging from one of them to the other and back again.

The hunk opened his mouth, then closed it again.

The older man supplied, "He's Daniel."

4

"Okay," the hunk agreed.

Was she still too out of it to hear that right?

"You just gave him a name?" Amelia asked.

The older man flushed. "Well, a code name, you know."

"Why?"

Daniel jumped back into the conversation. "We've had sabotage here lately. And an innocent-looking woman like you could be a decoy, sent to make us let down our guard."

REBECCA YORK

CHAPTER TWO

Amelia blinked. "That's … that's ridiculous," she sputtered, trying to focus. "You think I got caught in an avalanche so I could lure you away from … your job?"

"Yeah, like a suicide bomber," Daniel shot back.

The old guy clicked his tongue. "Daniel, don't you think that's going a little far?" Before the hunk could answer, the older man explained, "He's ex-FBI and a good man to have on the team—but he can be pretty intense."

FBI? Could this have anything to do with the phone call she'd gotten earlier? But how could it?

As Amelia tried to cope with the insanity of the conversation, she was thinking she should get away from these guys. When she tried to push herself up, her fingers dug into the hay and pressed against what felt like fabric. Wondering what was buried there, she started to pull it out. But the two men were already helping her to her feet.

"Do you have a code name too?" she asked the older guy.

"You can call me Nick," he answered as he put an arm around her shoulder and led her out of the stall.

But in the corridor, she stopped.

6

"Wait."

"Why?" Daniel asked.

"They're trying to talk to me."

"Who?"

The animals."

"Reindeer," Daniel said, confirming her earlier impression. "They can't speak."

"They're talking to each other," she countered.

Daniel shook his head. "If you say so."

"Let me stay here for a while."

"You don't think I'm going to leave you alone, do you?"

"Apparently not," she muttered.

Outside, the snow had stopped, transforming the scene into a beautiful winter evening. Like a painting on a Christmas card, Amelia thought as she raised her face to the sky where stars twinkled in the silken blackness. Once again, she heard holiday music floating on the wind, but now she was sure it was real, along with tempting aromas like cinnamon, cloves and ginger in the air.

She could see now that the stable was on the edge of a much larger complex. Had she somehow landed at a western ski resort? She revised that speculation when she spotted a big building—larger than a big-box store. Giant warehouse doors were open, and Amelia could see rows of benches where men were working—not at an assembly line but making what looked like individual toys. She caught glimpses of dollhouses, bikes, train sets, hobbyhorses, and a whole lot more. The workmen all seemed to be men in the prime of life. And not a woman was in sight. She might have said something about equal opportunity employment, but she'd figured out that it was better to keep her mouth shut until she learned more about this place. Pressing her lips together, she followed her guides.

In addition to the toy makers, workers carried stacks of boxes or operated forklifts, lifting cartons to high shelves.

And other groups of men sat relaxing at side tables eating cookies and drinking hot chocolate.

Nick saw her eyeing them. "During the busy season, they work in shifts. This is one of the dinner breaks."

"Cookies and hot chocolate for dinner?"

"My wife's cookies are very nourishing."

"Of course," she answered, humoring him.

They trooped past the workshop toward a cute little dwelling that looked like something out of a German fairy tale. Curlicued wooden cutouts decorated the eaves under the peaked roof. The windowpanes were diamond shaped, and the walk leading to the front door was paved with round stepping stones in lollipop colors. As she drew closer, she saw that the door looked like a slab of chocolate with decorative striped hinges fashioned to resemble candy canes.

Nick pulled the door open, and they stepped into a small entry. To the right was a big country kitchen where Amelia saw a little rounded woman with her gray hair done up in a bun. She was wearing a gingham dress covered by a frilly white apron. The scent of spices and butter wafted toward them.

"Just a minute. I've got to get these out," she called to the group, bending to open the oven door of a large old-fashioned stove. As it swung wide, Amelia felt a blast of heat.

The woman reached inside with mitted hands and pulled out a baking sheet of cookies. After setting the tray down on the stove top, she transferred the cookies to a cooling rack, then sprinkled on green colored sugar from a glass shaker. The counters around her were filled with round metal tins, all decorated with holiday scenes. Most were already brimming with cookies.

When the woman looked up from the task, she seemed surprised to see they had a visitor.

"This is Amelia Parsons," Nick says. "Daniel found her out in the snow."

"Nice to meet you. I'm Wendy ..." She stopped and glanced at Nick.

"Claus," he supplied.

Amelia couldn't help wondering if the guy was in charge of everybody's name.

Wendy tipped her head to the side and studied Amelia with a critical eye. "It looks like you had a bit of a bad time."

"Yes," she answered. This was the first woman she'd seen since arriving. And she seemed friendly. Was she going to be an ally?

The older woman continued to give Amelia a close inspection. "I think you could use some nourishment," she said, gesturing her guest to a wooden table that could seat a dozen. Amelia flopped into a chair, unbuttoned her coat, and draped it over the chair back.

"You too," Wendy said to Nick and Daniel.

The men sat, and the hostess brought over a platter of cookies. "I baked gingerbread, thumbprint cookies, date and nut squares, and some melt-in-your mouth shortbreads this morning," she said.

"They sound wonderful," Amelia answered "All the same one my grandma made."

She reached for one off the shortbreads and took a bite. Wendy was right; it melted in her mouth with a wonderfully buttery flavor that could have come straight from heaven.

"This is fantastic."

Her hostess beamed at the compliment. When she came back to the table, she was carrying a tray with four red mugs, each decorated with snowflakes on the sides. The enticing aroma of hot chocolate drifted up from the mugs.

Amelia took a cautious sip. The drink was nicely warmed but not too hot. To go with it, she took another cookie—a perfectly spiced gingerbread man. And as she ate, she had to acknowledge the truth of what Nick had told her. The cookies and chocolate were not only delicious, they were like eating health food that had an immediate invigorating effect. In fact, it wiped the last of the fog from her brain.

Amelia glanced up to see Nick watching her with a speculative look.

"Tell me again. How did you end up here?"

"I don't know," she answered. "It just happened. One minute I was crossing the street in town, and in the next minute I was out in the woods beyond the stable." A sudden zing of panic shot through her. "And I don't know how to get home."

"Well you must be here for a reason, dear," Wendy said. She took a sip of her chocolate and smiled. "Thank you for giving me an excuse to take a break."

Amelia murmured a quiet acknowledgment as she looked around the unlikely group. Nick had mentioned his wife, and they looked like a longtime married couple. But she wasn't sure how Daniel fit into the picture. He had the probing gaze and the tough-guy look of a security agent. Yet the way he acted with the old couple gave her the impression that there was a tenderness at his core. Or was she just making that up?

"Nick says you're ex-FBI," she ventured.

"Yeah."

She looked around the cozy kitchen, then back at Daniel.

"What are *you* doing here?"

"I'm on a special assignment," he answered, his clipped tone conveying that he wasn't prepared to discuss the details.

"Okay." She reached for another cookie to cover the feeling of being rebuffed.

Before she could take a bite, the rising and falling of a siren split the air.

CHAPTER THREE

Both Nick and Daniel jumped up, grabbed their coats and ran for the door.

Amelia looked at Wendy in alarm. "What's happening?"

The older woman shook her head. "I don't know, dear, but we should wait for the men to get back. They'll tell us."

She gave Wendy a startled look. "You don't want to see for yourself?"

"I'd just be in the way. This is men's business."

"Well, I can't just sit here." Amelia reached for her coat and pulled it on.

"Wait," the older woman called as Amelia sprinted for the door. The siren had stopped, but out in the snow, she could see the two men racing for the workshop.

She followed. When she'd last looked inside, it had been neat and orderly, with each man going about his business. Now the whole place had been transformed into a scene of chaos. Back in the area of the large shelves, a pile of washing-machine-sized boxes was scattered across the floor. From the middle of the pile, a pair of legs and booted feet protruded. Men were working together to lift the boxes and pull them off the unfortunate guy at the bottom of the pile. Daniel and Nick joined them.

When the rescuers lifted away the last box, she saw the unfortunate victim lying on the floor, his body bloody and battered. One of the other men rushed to his side, chafing his hand.

"What happened?" she gasped out.

"Boxes fell on him."

"I see that. But how?"

"Don't know."

Daniel ran for a first aid kit and brought it back.

A man nearby to her turned his head and looked at her, then whispered something to the guy next to him; and some kind of message she couldn't hear got passed on. Men turned to glance at her and then away.

And as she watched, she saw the crowd of onlookers close ranks around their injured fellow so that she could barely make him out. Still, she was aware that something strange was happening. It looked like the guy was fading away where he lay on the floor. She couldn't see his head, but she clearly saw his shirt go from bright red to muted orange and then gauzy, like the reverse of one of those old Polaroid photos that starts out blank but intensifies in color and clarity as the picture emerges.

No, that couldn't be happening she told herself. It must be a trick of the light.

Some of the crowd began to disperse, and she could still see the heavy boxes lying on the floor, but the injured man was gone. Maybe they took him to the infirmary?

As the workmen headed for their stations, Daniel called them back together.

REBECCA YORK

"Hold up. Did anyone see what happened?" he asks.

"I was busy at my workbench," one answered. Others agreed.

"Just like last time," Daniel muttered.

"Yeah," came a chorus of agreements.

"Some of you were eating dinner," Daniel prompted.

"On the other side of the room," a man pointed out.

Daniel walked to the spot where the man had been lying and looked up toward an empty gap on a high shelf.

"The boxes came from up there?" He pointed.

"Looks like it," someone answered.

"And who put them up there?"

Nobody seemed quite sure.

Daniel tried a different tack. "Okay, was there someone here you didn't recognize?"

"I might have seen someone," a short, thin guy with a red knit cap answered.

"Who?"

"Just a guy I didn't recognize."

As Amelia listened to their conversation, it sounded like this wasn't the first time there had been an accident in the workshop recently.

Daniel spotted her, and strode over. "Eavesdropping?" he asked.

"Something like this has happened before?"

Nick came around the end of one of the big shelving units. "Yes," he answered. "That's why Daniel's here—to investigate."

"You hired him?"

"He was assigned here," Nick said.

"And I wasn't doing my job," Daniel cut in, his gaze falling on Amelia. "I should have been keeping watch,

14

not eating cookies and drinking hot chocolate in the kitchen. But you lured me away."

She stared at him openmouthed, hardly able to believe what she was hearing. He was doing it again—making this her fault.

"Listen, I didn't ask to come here. I'm sorry if you think this accident has something to do with me."

"It wasn't an accident," Daniel snapped.

"How do you know?"

"Experience. Plus, I wouldn't be here if there was no external threat." Daniel stopped short, apparently noticing that they were drawing a crowd.

"Let's go back to the house," he muttered and glanced at a worried looking Nick.

"I have to stay to clean up," the older man said. "But you go on."

It looked like Daniel wanted to say something more, but he only gave Nick a quick nod before turning toward the door.

"Come on," he said to Amelia.

As he firmly took her arm and led her back the way they had come, she had to trot to keep up with him.

"I know you're angry and frustrated," she said.

He gave her an annoyed look. "How do you know?"

"It's obvious from your face. You want to find out how those boxes fell, and nobody can give you any information."

He dragged in a breath and let it out, and she knew he was struggling not to come back with some cutting rejoinder. "I'll try not to let my emotions show."

"What else has gone wrong here recently?"

"Other accidents," he snapped

They had reached the house. But instead of going in the front door, he led her around the side, into what she'd call a mud room. Coats hung on pegs on the wall, and boots were lined up under a bench.

They stepped through another door into a hallway that seemed to lead to the back of the house. But she couldn't be sure because it was long, with several twists and turns. As he ushered her along the corridor, she realized that the house was much bigger than it had looked from the outside.

They passed a lot of doors. Daniel peered into some of the rooms and closed the doors before she could get a look at what was inside, but finally he came to one that satisfied him.

"In here."

When she followed him inside, she found herself in a cozy bedroom that might have belonged to a wilderness lodge. The furniture was dark pine, with a narrow bed, a chest of drawers and a rocking chair in one corner. The spread on the bed looked like a lovely antique quilt. And a rag rug lay on the wide pine boards of the floor.

"Stay here. And stay out of trouble," Daniel said.

Before she could object, he stepped out of the room, and she heard a lock click.

When she rushed to the door and tried to turn the knob, it was definitely locked.

"Damn you," she whispered. "I want to help, and you're treating me like a criminal."

She looked around at her surroundings again. There was no TV and no telephone. Too bad she couldn't dial 911 and ask for help. Or did they even have 911 here?

There was a window opposite the door, and she crossed to it, lifting the shade. She had a view of the woods and the pine trees outside, but when she tried to open the window, she found it was also locked, with a mechanism she couldn't open. And when she pressed her fingers against the glass, it felt very solid, more like forged steel. So much for thinking she was going to climb out.

With a sigh, she sat down on the bed, wondering how long Daniel was planning to leave her here. Or maybe Wendy would show up with a care package of cookies and hot chocolate. And she could try asking the older woman some questions.

Daniel strode back down the hall, trying not to think about the woman he'd just locked in a bedroom. He was supposed to be working on an important case, but it was almost impossible to keep his thoughts from turning back to Amelia. She was a distraction he didn't need.

 Over the years, he'd had a lot of these special assignments, and he'd always gotten to the root of the problem. This time was different. There was something going on that he couldn't figure out. And Amelia's showing up here wasn't helping.

It had been a long time since he'd thought about a woman in any kind of intimate terms. Really, he'd been glad to focus on his work. But somehow Amelia had gotten under his skin, right from the first time he'd held her in his arms.

He'd been out doing a perimeter search, and when he'd first set eyes on her tramping through the snow, he'd been instantly sure that she didn't belong in this place.

He could have called out and demanded to know what she was doing there. Instead he'd opted for a covert approach. He'd been slipping over to apprehend her when he'd heard the avalanche and seen it bearing down on her. He'd gone into rescue mode, running like a maniac to scoop her up and carry her out of danger. And in those first moments when he'd held her, he'd been overwhelmed with tender feelings that he'd pushed aside for years.

When he'd brought her out of the cold into the stable and gotten a good look at her, she'd taken his breath away with her heart-shaped face and her wide blue eyes. And her blond hair had been a perfect complement to her ivory skin.

He made a snorting sound. She might be an innocent. She might be telling the truth as far as she knew it, but that didn't mean someone hadn't sent her here to get in the way of his investigation.

Yeah, if anyone were looking for the perfect woman to muddle up his thinking processes, it would be her.

Of course, he had an excellent way to do some checking on the story she'd given him.

His brows knitted in a scowl, he hurried down the hall to his office, stopped to unlock the door, and stepped inside, closing the barrier behind him. He knew Nick didn't approve of this place, which was why he kept the door locked.

There were no windows, a precaution against prying eyes. The room was furnished like one of his old government offices with a metal desk, a state-of-the-art computer, and a comfortable chair. He knew Nick was suspicious of modern technology, but Daniel knew it had definite uses.

He touched the keyboard, and the computer screen sprang to life. Sitting down in the office chair, he typed in Amelia Parsons, St. Stephens, Maryland.

After a few seconds a listing with her picture came up, and he saw it was the same woman.

She had said she owned a shop in town. And that checked out. It was called The Wild Side. He smiled when he saw the name. Going to her Web site, he looked at some of her merchandise. She had a lot of cute stuffed animals that looked like they'd been made by local craftsmen and other merchandise that must have been imported. She also had wild blackberry jelly, wild rose soap and paintings that featured nature scenes from the local area.

Going back to her bio, he saw that she was a member of the local merchants' association as well as on a committee that provided volunteer services to a local hospital. And she also taught some craft classes in her store.

From the local papers, he found that there had been a series of robberies of shops in the small towns on Maryland's Eastern Shore. One of them had been at Amelia's shop. Apparently she was the only merchant who had walked in on the burglar, and she'd given a description of the thief.

He stroked his chin, thinking of the consequences for her. She'd said she'd been hit by a car. Was that an attempt to eliminate a witness?

He went to another section of his database—a feature that would be unavailable to anyone but his level of special agent. His fingers hovered over the keyboard as he decided where to start. Finally he chose age five.

The screen blurred for a few seconds. Then he saw a scene like a video clip of a little girl in a classroom of kindergartners. She was sitting in a circle on the floor, singing along with the teacher who was teaching them Here Comes the Sun. He smiled as he watched her getting the lyrics. He exited the scene and scrolled through her life, fast forwarding, looking for her to do something like cheat on a test or shoplift.

He saw scenes of a happy family around the kitchen table, small-town events like picnics and barn dances. The most incriminating things he saw were her smoking out behind a barn with other kids and taking quarters from her mother's bureau drawer to use in a gumball machine that gave out little plastic prizes along with the gum. Sometimes he scrolled past several months. Other times he dipped back into her life in more detail.

He caught his breath as he saw her at sixteen making out with a boy. He didn't want to watch, but he couldn't turn away as he waited to find out if she'd sleep with the jerk. He was relieved to see she didn't let him get past second base.

Second base. He hadn't used that expression in a long time.

He was about to move the timeline forward again when a chime rang on his computer, and he looked at a silent alarm system he'd set up earlier.

As he saw the reading, he clicked off his computer and stepped back out of his office.

Amelia had had enough. Daniel might have tried to keep her out of the way, but she wasn't going to take it lying down. She walked over to the door, twisting the knob again with no results. Then she saw that there was a hole in the middle of the knob, like on the door to her bedroom when she'd been a kid. To unlock the door, all you had to do was stick something stiff into the hole and poke around until you found the mechanism.

She went back to the bedside table and started looking for something she could use. In the drawers were various things like nail files and nail scissors, ribbons, candy wrappers and string. She had almost given up on finding anything useful when she came across a wooden toothpick someone had left. Was it sturdy enough?

She guessed she'd find out. Inserting the wooden shaft in the lock, she pressed. The end of the toothpick broke off, and she couldn't hold back a small curse. Then she tried again, and this time the door clicked.

Elated, she opened the barrier and stepped into the hall which seemed to stretch endlessly in front of her.

There were rooms on either side, and she wondered what Daniel hadn't wanted her to see. All of the chambers were dark, and she had to flip the light switch to see what was inside. Some of the rooms were empty, and she ignored them. Others were bedrooms similar to the one she'd just left.

Doggedly, she kept opening doors, until she came to one room where there seemed to be no light switch. When she leaned in to feel along the wall, she lost her balance and started to tumble down a steep flight of stairs.

CHAPTER FOUR

Amelia screamed as she felt herself toppling into space. With the lights off she couldn't even see a railing to grab.

But before she'd fallen more than a few steps, strong arms caught her and hauled her back.

She knew who it was as soon as he pulled her to him.

"Daniel?" she asked as they stood in the dark at the top of the stairs.

"Yeah."

"Where did you come from?"

"Down the hall. What are you doing out here?"

She raised her chin. "I wasn't going to be banished like a naughty child."

"Do you ever do what you're told?" he asked in an exasperated voice.

"Not when it makes no sense."

His hands tightened on her shoulders as he moved her out of the dark and into the corridor. Now she could see his face—and his dark eyes glaring down at her. "You've been driving me crazy since you arrived, woman."

She'd often had the bad habit of responding to a challenge with defiance. "Good."

"What's that supposed to mean?"

"I think it's what you need. Or, I guess you could say that you have to be shaken up."

"That's a pretty smug comment."

"It's clear you're getting nowhere with your investigation. You need someone with a totally fresh imagination to help you," she argued.

"This isn't about imagination."

"So you say."

"Stop talking back to me," he ordered, his voice turning to an angry growl.

"Make me."

"All right." For a charged moment, his gaze locked with hers, and she would have backed away if she could have wrenched herself out of his solid grasp. She forgot about escape as he bent toward her mouth. There was a fleeting moment when she was too shocked to move. Then she nuzzled her lips against his. His mouth had looked so hard and uncompromising. But his lips were actually soft and inviting.

He made a sound deep in his throat as he gathered her closer, his hands moving up and down her back as he turned his head first one way and then the other, feasting on her like a starving man who had finally found sustenance.

And it was the same for her. Her life had been focused around building her business and cultivating the right contacts in St. Stephens. Ages had passed since she'd met a guy she wanted to kiss, but the moment she'd seen this man, she'd wondered what his mouth would feel like against hers.

Now she knew, and the sensation was electric, sending sparks through her body.

She forgot where they were, forgot everything except the man who was holding her in his arms, kissing her. And just as she thought they were never going to stop, she felt him pull away.

Her eyes blinked open, and she stared up at him in confusion.

"What's wrong?"

"I'm not here for my own indulgence."

"I know. You have a job to do," she repeated what he'd said more than once.

"Exactly."

A noise in the hall made them both turn. When she saw Nick striding toward them, she felt her cheeks redden. At least Daniel had stopped kissing her before they were discovered in a compromising position.

"I was just looking for you," Nick said.

"For me?" she asked.

"Well, you and Daniel."

She gave the chief investigator a triumphant look. "Nick wants my help."

When Daniel made a dismissive sound, Nick ignored him.

"I was getting ready to go over the records of all the guys working at the workshop. And I need a little help. Somebody has been sabotaging the operation. We're in an isolated location. People can't just wander in here."

That was Daniel's cue to focus on Amelia. "Except you."

"Don't start that line of reasoning again."

Before Daniel could send her back to her room, Nick put a hand on his shoulder. "I was thinking that maybe she's supposed to be here."

She smirked at Daniel. He scowled back at her.

"Let's see what we can figure out together," Nick said, emphasizing the last word.

Daniel didn't look happy, but apparently he wasn't going to keep arguing with the boss.

"Where are we going?" Amelia asked.

"My office."

In the next moment, Daniel reverted back to his one-track attitude. "You're taking her *there*?" he asked, sounding like Nick was going to initiate her into the workings of a secret cult.

"I think it's time."

"This is on you," Daniel said.

"That's right."

They followed Nick down the hall to a side corridor, and he unlocked the first door on the right.

When they stepped into his office, she couldn't believe what she was seeing. It was a mess, with papers and folders on every surface. To her eye, it looked like something out of a Charles Dickens novel. The most prominent piece of furniture was a massive old-fashioned roll-top desk littered with file folders and loose-leaf notebooks. More folders were stacked on what looked like an old library table along the wall. Next to it were wooden file cabinets, some with the drawers partly open. She riffled through some and saw that they were written in—Greek?"

"Why are these in Greek?" she asked.

"Greece is where I come from," Nick said.

She gave him a long look, trying to see his origins in his features.

"But that's not important now."

There were three chairs in the room—two at the long table and one at the desk. "You can take the desk."

Amelia sat down in the wooden rolling chair and almost fell over backwards when the mechanism tipped her back. She had to grab the edge of the desk to stay upright.

"Sorry," Nick said. "I'm used to it."

She nodded and reached for a notebook, being careful not to tip the chair again. The loose-leaf was stuffed with messy order forms from places all over the world—Russia, Germany, France, the U.S. Other books were similar. And when she turned to the folders, she found they contained personnel records.

"No computers?" she asked.

"I don't like 'em," Nick said. "I don't get all that stuff about passwords and spreadsheets."

"I offered to teach you," Daniel said.

"A waste of time. I've got more important things to do. And why would I need that stuff?"

"Because you're under some kind of attack," Daniel shot back.

"How would passwords help?"

They went back and forth for a few moments, and Amelia could see they'd had this argument more than once. She could also see that these two men liked and respected each other, even if they had a basic disagreement about work methods. It was fascinating to watch them, and she refrained from jumping in and saying that perhaps the filing system was part of the problem. How could anyone possibly keep his business straight in this mess?

Finally Daniel looked at Amelia in mock exasperation. "It's hard to get an old dog to accept new technology."

"This technology has worded fine for hundreds of years."

"Hundreds?" she asked

"Uh huh."

"Your father and grandfather ran this business?"

He grinned. "Well, you can say it's been in the family for generations."

Daniel interrupted her questions by plopping a pile of folders in front of her. "This is the paperwork on some of the men who recently arrived. See if you can find anything useful."

"What am I looking for?"

"I guess you'll know it when you find it. If you find it."

He and Nick sat down at the table with more folders and began opening them and thumbing through the paperwork.

To get an idea of what she might want to flag, she opened several folders and scanned through the material. Like the entries in the orders notebooks, the personnel files seemed to include men from all over the world. They had worked at various occupations. Some were doctors, some lawyers, others plumbers or farmers. So what were they doing in this place making toys?

Each file contained a notation of at least one personal incident that made her cringe. One guy had changed his name and moved away to avoid paying child support. Another had hit a dog with his car and sped away. Another had sold trailers that were vulnerable to tornado damage. Not only that, each file ended with a notation of how the man had died—

everything from heart attack to car crash to stroke to "old age."

She looked up to see both Nick and Daniel watching to judge her reaction.

"Is this right? The files say each of these men died."

"Yes," Nick answers. "Each of them did something in life that they had to atone for. There are many places of atonement. This is one of them."

She stared at him, trying to take that in. Then her gaze swung to Daniel. "You too?"

"Yes."

"What did you do?"

His mouth hardened, but he kept his gaze steady. "I was going to meet with a scumbag in New Jersey who had information about a terrorist plot. It turned out to be an ambush. A kid got caught in the cross fire and died."

"You shot him?"

"No."

"Then how was it your fault?"

She saw deep pain sweep across his chiseled features. "I was in too much of a hurry to set up the meeting. I should have been more careful about the place—and about my contact."

"You're being pretty hard on yourself."

He glared at her. "You weren't there. What do you know about it."

"I ... know you."

He snorted and stood, then stomped out of the room, leaving her and Nick alone.

Dealing with Daniel's revelation would have been hard enough. But there was so much more to absorb.

28

She pressed her hand against her forehead, feeling the way she had when she'd first found herself in the woods on the other side of the barn. It was like a giant wall of snow was crashing down on her, only now there was no physical danger.

She turned to the older man, trying to process everything that had happened since the beginning and seeing it in a new light. In a shaky voice, she asked, "Is this ... Santa's workshop?" She hitched a breath. " I mean the real Santa's workshop. Not some movie set or something."

"Yes. And the men here are my elves, although they don't look like the traditional picture."

Still grappling with this reality, she stared at the little man with the bushy white beard, "And you are Santa?"

"Yes."

"And that means Wendy is Mrs. Santa?"

"Yes."

A shiver went through her. "If all that's the truth, how did I get here? Did I do something bad, too?"

Nick shook his head. "I doubt it. In the first place, elves don't arrive out in the snow beyond the barn. They come to an intake area at the back of the warehouse where they go through orientation and get their assignments. And only men come here to work off their penitence."

That left a big question. "Then why am I here?"

Santa put a reassuring hand on her shoulder. "Obviously you have another purpose."

CHAPTER FIVE

Amelia waited with her breath frozen in her lungs for Santa to answer the big question hanging in the air.

"I think it could be what you said. You're supposed to help us solve a problem we can't solve for ourselves."

She nodded, thinking about the implications. "So why is your workshop under attack?"

Nick sighed. "It's part of an age-old struggle. The forces of evil have always been aligned against Christmas. This is simply the latest attempt."

"The forces of evil?" she asked in a shaky voice. "That sounds so ..." She raised one shoulder. "I don't know ... big."

He tipped his head to the side, studying her. "You don't believe in evil?"

She had never thought about it in such black and white terms. Bad things happened in the world, but she hadn't thought of it as a universal struggle. "I guess," she answered, her voice not quite steady.

"It's dangerous to ignore it. Evil has been in the world since the beginning of time. Well, since the snake tempted Eve to eat the apple of knowledge. We can fight it, but it pops up in different places. Like here."

Amelia nodded, trying to take it all in. She had been hit by so many revelations that her head felt like it was going to explode. It was hard to believe any of it, but she had the evidence of her own eyes.

"I need to ... think about all this," she whispered.

"I understand," the old man said gently. "You've had a lot to deal with lately."

Her first thought had been to go back to her room and lie down—if she could find it. She'd just had a couple of bad shocks. But as she walked slowly down the hall, she stopped short. What was wrong with her? Was she going to wimp out on Santa—when he'd told her she was here to help him?

Setting her jaw, she reversed directions, looking for the side entrance to the house. She found it in a few moments and stepped into the cold. She'd arrived in what she now thought of as Santaland at night with stars twinkling in a midnight sky above her. Now it was bright daylight on a clear winter day. But it was almost as cold.

She looked around at the frozen landscape, at the tree branches covered with ice and the snow on the roofs of the buildings. At home, days after a blizzard, the snow turned dirty. Here it apparently stayed pristine white. It looked as beautiful as it had at night, but what would it be like to live in this cold world all year long?

Shivering, she buttoned her coat and headed for the huge workshop building. When she stepped through the big doors, the scene was a lot like the first time she'd seen the place, with men dressed in bright Christmas colors busy making toys. But now that she had some insight into their backgrounds, the scene didn't look

31

quite as cheerful. Every one of these workers had done something questionable in his lifetime.

But the upbeat holiday music was still playing, and men were still taking their cookie and chocolate breaks.

She headed for the work area, walking among the men, trying to get a sense of who they really were.

None of them looked like what she'd think of as evil. But why would they. If they didn't fit in, they'd be out of here pretty quickly.

All of them appeared industrious—like they were determined to make amends for what they'd done in life. She should have asked Nick how long they had to stay here—but she'd been too off balance to think of all the right questions.

As she went up and down the rows, she paused to look over the worker's shoulders. Many of them hummed along with the music, seemingly lost in the task they were performing.

Others gave her little glances, definitely aware that they were being scrutinized. But most of them paid her no attention as they went about their tasks.

All the men looked like they were sticking to their duties—both the toy makers and the guys who were operating the forklifts. But some of the workbenches were empty, and she figured that these were the men at the tables having their cookies and hot chocolate.

She moved out of the bright overhead lights and into the shadows by the side of a huge shelving unit. Everything went along with no interruptions.

Some men got up and went to the food table. Others came back to their stations. Finally from her position by the shelves, she saw one man acting suspicious. He was wearing a red and green plaid shirt, had an almost bald head, and was looking around every few seconds to see if anybody was paying attention to him. He must have decided nobody was watching because he slipped a rag doll under his shirt, then climbed out of his seat before heading toward the back of the workshop—to another line of storage shelves.

He'd definitely stolen a doll, she thought as she let him get out of sight before she followed him down the aisle. She got to the end of the row and looked around. At first she didn't know where he'd gone. Then she peered through a gap in the shelves and found him squatting on the floor next to a large box. As she watched, she saw him lift his shirt and stick the doll he'd taken into the box.

She had tried to be quiet, but he must have been super tuned for trouble. Looking up, he spotted her, and sick panic flashed across his face. In the next moment, he jumped up and ran in the other direction.

CHAPTER SIX

"Stop! What are you doing?" Amelia called out as the guy sprinted around the corner.

Afraid that he would get away, she put on a burst of speed, catching up with him just before he reached an exit at the back of the warehouse.

But now what was she going to do? Trying to prevent him from escaping, she leaped on his back. She had slowed him down. But he kept moving, dragging her along. She clamped her knees around his hips, banging on his back with her fists.

"Stop," she called out. "Stop."

Ignoring her, he kept struggling onward. He reached the door, threw it open and staggered into the night with her still on his back. Snow was falling again, and he lumbered through the drifts.

"Help. Daniel, help me. He's getting away."

The guy finally shook her off, and she landed in a snowbank. Before she had pushed herself up, he was already out of sight.

She tried to catch up, and when she rounded the corner, she saw that Daniel and Santa had both arrived and were wrestling with the culprit. They brought him down to the cold ground.

"No, please," he pleaded, trying to get away.

Santa held him while Daniel pulled a pair of handcuffs off his belt, When the man's hands were secured behind his back, Daniel turned to her. "What was he doing—besides trying to escape?"

"Stealing toys."

"No," the man protested.

Amelia looked up to see that dozens of workers had come outside and had surrounded the group.

Santa looked up, too. "You all go back to your stations," he said. "We're already behind schedule."

Some of the men scuffled their feet, but most of them started back to the warehouse.

Santa waited until the crowd had dispersed. "What's your name?" he asked.

The man glanced around at the three people who had brought him down. "I guess I can't hide it. I'm Clyde Fuller."

"That name mean anything to you?" Santa asked Daniel.

He shook his head.

"I'll show you what he was doing," Amelia said. She led the way back into the building, with Daniel hustling Fuller along and Santa guarding his rear.

She took them to the place where Fuller had secreted his box of toys. In addition to the doll, there was a set of plastic building pieces, action figures from a popular comic series turned feature movie, terry-cloth blocks and a child's doctor kit.

Santa riffled through the contents of the box. "These are workshop property," he said, his voice gruff. What are you planning to do with any of this?"

The man hung his head. "What happens to my family if I tell you?"

"What does your family have to do with this?" Daniel demanded.

There were tears in the man's eyes. "I died in a robbery a few weeks ago, trying to get money for my family. I know they're going to have an awful Christmas, with me gone and all, and I was trying to collect some toys for my kids."

"Oh come on," Daniel said.

"No wait," Santa answered, "We can check that out."

He led the way back to the extension of the house and then to his office, where they all waited while he shuffled through folders on his desk.

"Fuller, Fuller," he muttered as he looked for the right folder.

Finally he found it, and read the first page. "He's only been here a few weeks. That checks out." He flipped to the last page. "Yes, it says he robbed a bank to get money for his family."

"There are better ways to do that," Daniel observed.

"But I couldn't find none," the man answered.

"I can find out if he's being straight with us," Santa said, putting a hand on the man's shoulder and pressing hard. The man went rigid, and Santa shifted his hand to the man's temple. They both stood with their eyes closed for long moments. A wealth of expressions crossed Fuller's face, everything from hope and ecstasy to despair and back again. As she watched, Amelia knew that something supernatural was taking place.

Finally, Santa's eyes blinked open. "He's telling the truth. He was worried about his family the whole time he was here. And he was still trying to do something for them—even if he wasn't going about it the right way. Santa shook his head. "But I see from his mind that he doesn't have a clear concept of what's right and what's wrong."

Daniel pulled out a key and unlocked the cuffs, looking like he wished he hadn't been so rough on the guy.

"What are we going to do?" he asked in a husky voice.

"I can arrange a special shipment of toys to his family," Santa said.

"You can?" Fuller asked, his voice wavering between shock and relief.

"Yes. I still try to do business in the old way, but it's not always possible—there are simply too many households and not enough chimneys. And those newfangled ones with the gas logs are awful. When they put them in, they do something that makes the opening way too narrow."

Amelia saw that Daniel's eyes were misty, and she knew he had been affected by the man's story.

"What are you gonna do to me?" Fuller asks. "Are you gonna report me for this?"

Santa kept his gaze steady. "Not if you go back to your job and stay out of trouble."

"Oh, thank you, sir," Fuller gasped out.

"Go on now."

The man scuttled away, leaving the three of them in the office.

"I'm sorry. I thought he was the one causing all the trouble," Amelia said in a low voice.

"A natural mistake," Santa said. "And you did him a big favor."

"How."

"Those toys never would have gotten to his family. He wasn't authorized to send a shipment. Plus, he was here to work off the fallout from that robbery. There's no way he'd be working anything off if he was still stealing."

Amelia nodded. "But I can't help feeling bad."

"If you keep watching, you may well figure out what's going on," Santa said. "But I have to get back to the warehouse. The men need to know how this came out."

"Wait," she said.

Santa turned to her with a questioning look.

"That thing you did when you put your hand on his temple. You didn't do it with me."

"I was pretty sure you were telling the truth."

"Thank you," she murmured.

He nodded and left her alone with Daniel. She might have pointed out that Santa had believed her, but she thought it was better to say, "I'm sorry about accusing that guy."

"Not your fault. You were looking for a worker doing something out of pattern, and you found it."

She nodded. "When you heard his story, you looked like you felt sorry for him."

"I did."

"One thing I like about you—you're adaptable."

"How?"

"You were ready to throw the book at him. Then you saw his point of view."

"Yeah. And now I have to get back to work—looking for the real culprit."

She wanted to continue the conversation. Or, to be honest, she wanted more than conversation, but he had shifted his focus back to his job. When he left, the office seemed very empty.

After demonstrating she was a total flop on her first covert mission, Amelia wondered what she was going to do now. Opening the door, she looked down the hall and saw Daniel disappear into a side corridor. Obviously, he didn't want her help—or anything else from her.

But as she stood in the open office doorway, the aroma of cinnamon and cloves wafted toward her. She stepped out, closed the door behind her, and walked down the hall, letting the tempting scents lead her to the kitchen.

Wendy Claus was transferring spice drop cookies from a cooling rack to one of the Christmas tins that sat on the counter. She looked up when she realized someone was watching.

"On your own again?" she asked, sympathy in her voice.

Amelia raised one shoulder in a kind of shrug. "It looks like it."

"Come in and sit for a spell."

Wendy wiped her hands on her apron and brought over an assortment of goodies, then went back for two mugs of hot chocolate.

Both women pulled up chairs at the wooden table.

Amelia looked around the kitchen that was brimming with mixing bowls, baking sheets, pans and decorative tins.

"I guess baking so much keeps you pretty busy."

Wendy swept her arm in a broad gesture, acknowledging the state of the kitchen. "It's not always so frantic around here. This is our rush season, and we take on extra workers—who have to be fed. But after Christmas, things will calm down for a few months. And Nick and I can relax together."

Amelia nibbled on a sugar cookie. "I guess you've been married for a long time."

"Centuries."

She blinked at the unexpected answer. "So, uh, he manages the factory, and you feed the workers?"

"Yes, but don't forget the Christmas Eve deliveries."

"Right."

Wendy took a sip of hot chocolate. "Nick's a hardworking man. But he plays hard, too, when we have some time to ourselves."

Amelia would have loved to ask more about Wendy and Nick's life, but she didn't want to pry.

Mrs. Claus's voice slipped into a faraway tone. "I knew I was taking on a big commitment when I married him."

"But you loved him."

"Yes."

"How did you meet?"

"In the forest." She smiled at some long-ago memory. "I ran with kind of a wild crowd. Nick wasn't one of us, but he'd come around sometimes. I sensed he was looking for a wife. I didn't really love the life I was leading, and when he started paying attention to me, I paid attention back. In those days, he wasn't near as busy. He just had to deal with a few countries. The job has grown over the years."

"I imagine."

Wendy set down her mug. "I've seen the way Daniel looks at you."

"With suspicion," Amelia answered.

"That's because of his special-agent job. I mean, he had to be suspicious when you dropped in out of nowhere. But I can see you spark something in him. He looks at you the way Nick looked at me all those years ago."

Was it true?

Wendy studied her expression. "Are you afraid to find out what he's feeling?"

"I don't even know where to find him."

"I think he's probably in his office."

"Which is where?"

Wendy laughed. "Right, the back of the house is a warren if you don't know your way around."

"When I looked out the door, I saw him go down a side corridor."

"Um hum." The older woman got up, reached for a small tin printed with holly garlands and handed it to Amelia. "Take him some cookies."

"Right. Good idea."

She pushed back her chair, picked up the tin and exited the kitchen, retracing her steps until she came to the side corridor she thought Daniel had taken. Clutching the container of cookies, she turned left and walked slowly, looking at the bottoms of the doors. When she came to one with a light shining underneath, she knocked.

"Who's there?" Daniel called out.

Without answering, she pushed the barrier open and stepped into an office that was quite different from Nick's.

Daniel stared at her in surprise while she glanced around the office, bemused.

"What are you doing here?" he asked from where he sat at a state-of-the-art desktop computer.

"Cookie delivery."

He stood up and took a step toward her. "I don't need any cookies."

"Of course you do."

She moved farther into the office and set the tin down on his desk. "How come Santa's office looks like a nineteenth century cartoon and yours looks like it could belong to Bill Gates?" she asked.

"Nick adapts slowly. I have no problem using modern technology."

She peered at the screen, where he'd called up information on the workers. It looked like the same material she'd seen in Nick's folder. "Do you have spy cameras in the warehouse?"

"No."

"Why not?"

"Nick said I couldn't go that far, and he's the boss."

"But it might make the difference in catching the ... mischief maker."

He sighed. "I know."

"Maybe he doesn't really want to find out."

"I thought of that. It's a problem."

He sounded weary.

"Are you working this case twenty-four seven?"

"Yeah."

"Maybe if you back off a little, it will help."

CHAPTER SEVEN

Daniel fixed her with a challenging look. "How?"

"Don't you ever try to think of something, and it won't come to you? Then you sort of put it out of your mind, and the answer pops into your head," she answered.

"Yeah," he admitted.

"Do that now," she advised.

She'd never thought of herself as aggressive with men, but she was pretty sure that if she let his acquired instincts take their course, Daniel would go back to work. To keep that from happening, she reached for him.

He drew in a quick breath as she circled his shoulders with one arm and cupped the back of his head with her free hand.

His mouth connected with hers, and she knew from the moment his lips touched down that he wasn't going to pull away. They were a man and a woman who wanted each other, and denial had fled from the picture.

Could she make things normal between them? She didn't know, not in this environment. Still she hoped she was projecting confidence.

"I like your reaction," she whispered as she slid her lips against his, then opened so that his tongue could play with the line of her teeth before gliding against her tongue.

Still, he pulled back a little and dragged in a breath before saying, "You're sure about this?"

"I wouldn't be here if I weren't sure." she answered, before going back to the more pleasurable part of the exchange.

When their lips finally broke apart, they were both trembling.

"I'm thinking we need to get off our feet," she murmured, looking around the office. "But I don't see a good place to do that."

"Well, this is the land of possibilities," he answered. As she watched, she saw the little office swirl around her as though it had been caught in a tornado, and she had to close her eyes to keep from getting dizzy. She felt the sensation of movement and hooked her hands over Daniel's shoulders because she needed to cling to something solid.

When the spinning finally stopped, she opened her eyes. To her astonishment, they were standing in a charming bedroom. It was like something out of an Irish fairy tale—a room in a stone cottage with a handmade quilt on the bed, a rag rug on the polished wood floor, and the warm glow of candles flickering on a dresser across from the bed.

"Where are we?" she asked.

"Somewhere I thought you'd like."

"I do," she answered, hearing the thickness of her own voice.

She still clung to him as she took in more of the surroundings, seeing an old-fashioned washstand with a blue china bowl and pitcher, a lace scarf on the dresser, and a stout wooden door.

The attention to detail made her look down at herself. Instead of her heavy winter clothing, she was wearing a translucent white gown with thin lacy straps. And when she focused on Daniel, she saw he had changed into a white shirt open at the neck and black trousers. Not a modern dress shirt but something old-fashioned with big sleeves and embroidery on the front.

The first two buttons of his shirt were open, and she saw dark hair poking out at the top.

She reached for the front of the shirt and opened two more buttons before slipping her hand inside.

"Nice. I like your chest. It's so broad and muscular." She laughed. "Although I think chest hair is supposed to be out—judging from the male models I've seen."

"You look at male models?"

She flushed. "I don't seek them out. They're in books I see online." Raising her face, she met his gaze. "But I sought *you* out."

His breath caught. "Why? I did my best to push you away."

"I know. But I decided not to let you."

His eyes glittered as he stroked her arms, her ribs, the indentation of her waist, the outside of her thighs. And everywhere he touched sent heat radiating through her body.

She moved restlessly against him. "Please," she gasped out.

"What do you want?"

"To join you in that charming bed."

He walked her backwards, then reached behind her to throw the spread and covers aside. They stood swaying together until he lifted her onto the horizontal surface and came down beside her.

The look in his eyes was enough to scald her, and their gazes locked as he reached for the hem of her gown.

"I want both of us to remember this," he said in a deep, sensual voice.

"Oh yes."

Afterwards, they clung together for long moments. As she settled down beside him, his hand stroked her arm. "Thank you,"

"Thank you for bringing me here."

"I wasn't looking for anything like that," he said, his voice thick with emotion.

She slid her lips against his shoulder. "I know. That's why I didn't let you back away from me when I brought the cookies to your office."

He laughed. "What man can resist a woman carrying cookies?"

"You're teasing me."

"Maybe a little, but I loved that you made the gesture."

She loved that he'd taken this time away from what he considered important work to be with her. She loved that he had finally let down his guard.

Now she wanted to ask how long they could stay here together, but she knew the question would be a mistake. He had made room for her in his Spartan life, and she didn't want to remind him that they were stealing time from a job that he took very seriously.

He'd told her so little about himself, and she wanted to find out more, but before she could figure out how to frame a question, he turned the tables on her, "Tell me how you ended up in the snow outside Santa's Workshop."

"I told you before."

"Back then I thought you were up to no good."

"I noticed."

"This time, I'm listening."

She could have let that get to her, but she was feeling too mellow for the words to sting.

Sitting up in bed she pulled the covers over her breasts. He sat up beside her, his gaze never leaving her face.

Feeling self-conscious, she looked down at her hands. "Okay. I was in St. Stephens, Maryland, where I live. I have a shop there called On the Wild Side that sells items made by local craftsmen and also from coops in third-world countries." She continued. "I was upset about a couple of things, and I wasn't paying attention when I crossed Main Street near my shop."

"Upset about what?"

"I'd gotten a call from the FBI about the robbery, and also I hadn't received a shipment of ornaments from a company called Santa's Workshop." She dragged in a breath and let it out. "I don't know if it was *this* Santa's Workshop. I mean, I don't know if you all ship directly to customers. But the ornaments were for the Christmas tree at the local hospital. I had volunteered to decorate it. I noticed you and Santa reacted to that."

"Yes, but I think it's not relevant now. I want to know about the call from the FBI. What did they want?"

"Around here, December is the busy season. Back home, the busy season is in summer when the resort towns on Maryland's Eastern Shore are flooded with tourists. We're not on the ocean, but we have a river and a lot of water activities. In July and August, when the shops were full of merchandise, someone was breaking into stores in our town and the ones nearby. I was the only merchant who saw the robber."

He sucked in a sharp breath. "How?"

"The robberies were at night when the shops were closed. I was home, but I had given my business card to a customer, a woman who had been in and seen a silver necklace that she liked. She hadn't decided whether to buy it or not. It was ten in the evening when she called me and said she wanted it and she was leaving for home in the morning."

"Not very considerate of her."

"Some people are like that. They only think about what they want—not what's convenient for you. I got dressed and went down to the shop to pick up the jewelry. When I got there, the back door was ajar, and I wondered if I'd forgotten to lock it. I knew it was a bad idea to go in, and I was about to call the cops when this guy came barreling out. He knocked me down and kept running, but I did get a look at his face before I went down. And I know his car was a Honda."

She could see he was listening intently.

"That's not so good for you if you're the only person who can identify the burglar."

"I guess you're right," she conceded.

"You talked to the police?"

"Yes, and I didn't hear anything about it for months. Then the FBI called."

"Then it's not a simple robbery."

"What is it?"

"I don't know."

"I think the agent wanted me to meet him, but the transmission had a lot of static, so I didn't catch his name."

He nodded. "How much was missing from your shop?"

"A shipment from Africa. I was so upset I forgot all about the jewelry the woman wanted. She left in the morning and never got the piece."

"Too bad for her."

They sat close together for long moments. He must have been in the mood to keep asking questions.

"How did you get into the craft shop business?"

"It was originally my mom's shop. I used to play there when I was little. Later, I'd do my homework in the back room," she answered, feeling a lump forming in her throat.

"And she's passed on?" Daniel asked gently.

"Yes. A few years ago. She had a heart condition."

"I'm sorry. What about your dad?"

"He was never really in the picture."

"That's rough."

"Mom made it work. And my Uncle Anthony—her brother—was like a dad to me."

"Is he still around?"

"Yes. He owns a charter fishing boat."

She had talked a lot about herself. Maybe she could switch topics now. "What about you?" she asked.

"What about me?"

"Where did you grow up?"

He laughed. "All over. My dad was in the Navy, and we were posted to a lot of different places. Did you know there are Navy bases that are nowhere near the water. Like Lemoore, California. It's in the San Joaquin Valley."

"I guess I never thought about that. I always lived in St. Stephens. Always near the water."

She laid her head on his shoulder. This time when he stroked her arm, she sensed a change in him.

CHAPTER EIGHT

Amelia closed her eyes as he spoke the words she had dreaded. "You know we can't stay here."

"Yes."

"I have to get back to work."

She swallowed hard, hoping she might be able to tempt him to stay in this charming cottage for a while longer.

His next words dashed that hope. "I'm not supposed to be taking time for myself."

She couldn't argue with him, even if his own guilt was driving him. And perhaps she had made that worse. Plus he had set the rules, or more likely it wasn't him. She should admire his sense of duty and his integrity; instead, she felt a deep pang as he climbed out of bed and reached for the clothing he'd left on the floor. He was dressed in under a minute. When he turned to face her, his expression was sad. She held out her arms to him, and he came back to the bed. For a long moment, he gathered her close, and then he turned and walked away.

Through a film of tears, she tried to focus on his broad shoulders. But she couldn't keep him in view. Sunlight streamed through the window in the other room, blurring his outline. Suddenly he was gone. Vanished.

She slid down in the bed and pulled the sheet up to her nose, breathing in his unique scent. The bed was still warm from his presence, but gradually it began to cool.

Knowing she couldn't simply stay here, she rose and picked up the gown she'd been wearing. When she'd put it on, she walked barefoot out of the bedroom. The main room of the house was a combination living area and kitchen, with rustic furniture and cooking equipment that looked even more primitive than Wendy Claus's. She walked around the room, picking up objects—a small china pitcher, a wooden spoon, a straw broom. All of them felt real.

She walked to the window, looking out at a lush green landscape dotted with rocks.

What would happen if she wanted to stay here? Probably not a good idea, she decided. But how did she get back to Santa's Workshop? She wasn't Dorothy in the Wizard of Oz, wearing a pair of magic shoes that she only had to click together to travel through time and space.

But she was in a fantasy location that Daniel had created. It wasn't real. And if she closed her eyes and willed herself back to Santaland, hopefully she'd get there.

She settled into a small rocking chair, pressing into the cushioned back and closing her eyes, imagining herself in Daniel's office. For long moments, it felt like she was just wasting her time. Was she going to be trapped here alone—until Daniel noticed she was missing and came back for her?

Then she felt the sensation of movement and squeezed her eyes tighter. Maybe because she'd been thinking about the Wizard of Oz, it was like a whirlwind had caught her up and was turning her around and around. She gripped the sides of the chair, praying that the wind wasn't going to sweep her off into space.

When the movement finally subsided, she cautiously opened her eyes. She was back in Daniel's office. And she was wearing the clothes she'd had on when she arrived in Santaland.

That was a relief, since running around here in a nightgown would be rather chilly—not to mention embarrassing.

She looked around the office and felt a little pang when she saw the cookie tin still sitting on the desk. As she'd anticipated, Daniel wasn't there. But she didn't need him to implement the idea she'd been mulling over back in the cottage.

She glanced over her shoulder, wondering if Daniel would be annoyed at her using his computer. But why should he, if she was trying to help him solve the workshop invasion problem?

When she touched the keyboard, the screen sprang to life. He was using a standard system, and she was able to access his file directory. She saw the personnel files and the work orders, as well as the information on whether something had been shipped. But she saw something else as well. There was also a file that said Reindeer.

She opened it, seeing notations on each of the animals. There were some who seemed to have been with Santa from the beginning, like Donner and Blitzen. Others like Rudolph had arrived later. And some had been added more recently. So why was there turnover in the herd?

Getting up, she walked down the hall toward the front of the house. When she reached the kitchen, Wendy Claus looked up from a batch of gingerbread men she was decorating with white piped-on icing.

The older woman gave her a close inspection. "I take it you connected with Daniel?"

Amelia felt her cheeks heat. "Yes." She raised her head, meeting Wendy's gaze. "We made love, and it was wonderful. And then he rushed off to get back to the investigation."

"He's driven."

"I'm hoping I can help him solve the mystery. Then he can relax."

Wendy tipped her head to the side. "It might not come out the way you expect."

"Why not?"

"What's happened here that you expected?"

Amelia dragged in a breath and let it out. "You have a point." Drifting to the counter, she looked into the tins and took out a thumbprint cookie. When she bit into it, she found it had an apricot center.

"What happens to all the mixing bowls and baking pans?" she asked.

"I have a dishwasher for them." She pointed to a set of double doors. It's behind there. Along with the washer and dryer."

"You have all that stuff?" she asked in surprise. "I thought Nick didn't like modern technology."

"He doesn't. But I told him that if there was a way to avoid endless dishwashing, I wanted it."

"I thought you deferred to him."

"I do, in a lot of things. Around here we have men's jobs and women's jobs. But there's no reason not to make life a little easier."

"Agreed." When she finished chewing, she said, "I was wondering about the reindeer."

"What about them?"

"Daniel had their records on his computer. Some have been here since you arrived. Others are more recent. How come?"

Wendy finished the gingerbread men. A mechanical timer went off, and she pulled a tray of shortbreads from the oven and set it on a rack.

"It's hard for the older ones to pull the sled with so many toys. We get newer recruits. And of course, Rudolph is special because of the song about him."

Amelia nodded. "Are they like the men in the workshop. Do they come here to work off something bad they did."

"No. They were never men. It's an honor for them to come here."

"Um hum." She walked among the boxes of cookies, found one with chocolate brownies and helped herself to one.

"I haven't been to the stables since I arrived. And there was something there I was curious about."

"What's that, dear?"

"Maybe nothing."

Leaving the kitchen, she headed for the front door, then out into the cold, where it took a few moments to orient herself. Then she spotted the barn roof and used it as a guide.

When she arrived at the main door, there was silence inside the barn, but as soon as she stepped inside, the reindeer started talking to each other as they had before. She stopped at several stalls, peering inside. Some of the animals looked back at her. Others swung their heads toward their neighbors. Were they trying to communicate with her? Or were they strictly talking to each other?

She walked slowly down the aisle between the stalls, heading for the one where Daniel had taken her that first night.

Inside, the pile of hay where she'd fallen was still there. She'd felt something buried in it, and she'd wanted to find out what it was, but Daniel and Santa had hustled her away before she'd been able to find out.

Crossing to the pile, she began to dig for the hidden piece of fabric. Her fingers found it moments later, and she pulled out the same kind of shirt the men in the workshop had been wearing. Digging farther down, she found a pair of pants and then some of the workmen's boots.

She spread them all out on the hay, studying them. They looked worn. What were they doing in here? Did workmen sneak into the barn and take naps when they were supposed to be making toys?

She turned to the nearest stall and saw one of the reindeer staring intently at her. He was the one she'd seen before with the red nose.

"Rudolph?"

He bobbed his head up and down enthusiastically, and she felt like they had actually communicated. But when he opened his mouth and started to speak, it sounded like he was babbling.

"I can't understand you."

He blinked his eyes and pawed he ground.

"You want to tell me something?"

He bobbed his head up and down, then made a braying sound that was more like a donkey than a reindeer.

When he pawed the ground more frantically, she looked at him helplessly. In the background the other reindeer were making a racket like a Greek chorus. And this time, in the middle of it, she thought she heard someone calling her name. Someone with a strangely accented voice.

He sounded insistent—as though he wanted to get her attention—but she didn't want to focus on him. She wanted the animals to quiet down and let her think.

"You're not helping," she shouted above the din.

They quieted, and she realized they could understand her, even if she couldn't understand them.

She turned back to the red-nosed beast. "Would it help if I let you out?"

He made the braying sound again and pumped his head up and down before banging his hooves against the wooden door.

Was it okay to open his stall? She hoped she wasn't doing the wrong thing when she lifted the latch. He dashed out of the enclosure and into the stall where she'd found the clothing and pawed the straw.

"Yes I know," she answered, pointing to the clothing.

Rudolph shook his head vigorously and kept pawing, then stamped on the ground.

"You want me to do it?"

He bobbed his head excitedly. She got on her knees and kept throwing straw out of the way. It looked like someone had dug a little tunnel through the hay, and as she followed it to the back wall, she saw a hole in the side of the barn down by the floor.

She turned to Rudolph. "A rat?"

He nodded, then shook his head.

"What do you mean?" she asked. "Is it a rat or not? And how could a rat be the cause of Santa's problems?"

Rudolph gave her a look that made her chest tighten. It was clear he desperately wanted to communicate, but he couldn't quite do it. She felt like she was in the middle of a game of charades, but she and the other player didn't quite speak the same language. And it seemed like the stakes were a lot higher than in any game she'd ever played.

With a sigh, she walked out of the stall. When she looked back at the reindeer, he stared at her, just as thwarted by their inability to communicate.

She slapped her hand against her thigh. "There's got to be a better way."

In answer, he stamped on the floor. Sadly, she shook her head.

"I'm just not getting it. Maybe I'd better go find Daniel and see if he can figure it out," she said.

Rudolph made a desperate bleating sound.

"I get that you want me to stay, but I just can't do that now. I'm sorry. You'd better get back in your stall."

His expression turned stubborn as he braced his legs against the floor and shook his head vigorously.

"Please," she coaxed. "I'm going to get in trouble if Santa or Daniel come in here."

She had never seen an animal sigh. But Rudolph did it. Then he turned and stepped back into his enclosure.

"Thank you."

He was still giving her a pleading look.

"I won't just go away. But I can't handle this myself she said to the clearly distressed animal.

Still, it was with a feeling of relief that she closed and locked the door behind him.

She hurried back to the workshop, but she didn't find Daniel inside. Some of the men were looking at her suspiciously. She ignored them and headed for Daniel's office. He wasn't there either.

Her panic rising, she ran back to the workshop.

This time she called out, "Has anyone seen Santa or Daniel?"

Men all over the room looked up. Most answered "no." And a few gave her hostile looks.

One muttered in a voice almost too low to hear, "Why did you come here to start trouble?"

"Me?" she answered in surprise. "I'm not the one causing trouble."

"Then who is?" the questioner asked in a menacing tone.

She stood her ground, wondering if the men were going to leap up and attack her as a scapegoat. Like in *Lord of the Flies*, where they picked a boy as a sacrificial victim. After all, the guys in this room were here because they had done something underhanded in life.

She waited tensely as low whispers filled the room. Finally one man said, "Santa was here a little while ago. I think he was going to the kitchen to get more cookies."

She let out a long sigh of relief, then called out, "Thanks," before turning and heading for the main house.

As she hurried along the path, she was thinking it didn't make sense to blame her. She hadn't even been here when the sabotage had started. It was already happening when she arrived. But perhaps it was natural to blame an outsider—and a woman at that.

She forgot about the accusations as she stepped into the kitchen and was confronted with a scene that curdled her blood.

CHAPTER NINE

Santa was lying on the floor, his face bloody, and Wendy and Daniel were kneeling on either side of him.

"What happened?" Amelia cried out as she started running across the room, then almost slipped on the strangely slippery floor. She grabbed wildly at one of the kitchen counters and managed to keep herself from falling.

"Careful." Daniel scrambled up and hurried to her side. For a long moment, their eyes locked, and she knew he was thinking about the time they'd spent together in the cottage—and his abrupt departure.

"Are you all right?" he asked in a thick voice.

"Yes," she answered, then looked back at Santa. "What happened?

"I came in and found him here," Wendy moaned. "He was lying on the floor."

"There was a big patch of cooking oil on the linoleum," she added. "I think it was meant to make me fall. Only I'd asked Nick to come in and take a delivery of cookies to the men."

"Or maybe someone realized he was coming here—and it was meant for him," Daniel suggested.

From the floor, Santa groaned, and everyone turned back to him.

"Nick, oh Nick," Wendy whispered as she chafed his hand.

"I'm okay," he answered in a gruff voice. When he tried to push himself up, Daniel put a hand on his shoulder.

"Stay down."

"I'm fine," Santa insisted. He looked from Wendy to Daniel and back again. "You remember when I fell off that steep roof with the loose tiles a few years ago? I was okay in a matter of hours."

"Yes," Wendy said.

"Help me sit up," Santa said.

Wendy hesitated.

When Santa persisted, Daniel helped him sit.

Wendy went to the sink, ran water on a clean dish towel and brought it back. Kneeling again, she began to wash the blood off her husband's face.

By the time she was finished, he was looking a lot better.

"You need a gingerbread cookie," she said. "They're the most nourishing."

"Okay," he agreed.

Daniel stood up and inspected the big oil splotch on the floor. "We need to put something over that—and wipe it up." He turned to Wendy, do you have more towels.

"Yes."

She got up, opened a deep drawer and pulled out a pile of terry-cloth towels. Daniel took them, scattered them over the oil and used his foot to wipe at the mess.

"Did you see anyone come in here?" he asked Wendy.

She looked distressed. "Nobody." Turning to Nick, she said, "I want you in your bed."

"I'm fine."

"In bed, now."

She was going to help him up when Daniel stepped in and gave the old man his hand.

Santa hauled himself to his feet and stood swaying on unsteady legs.

Wendy looked at Daniel and Amelia. "Help me make sure he gets to bed."

"Of course," they both said.

"I'm going to make sure the bed is nice and neat," Wendy called over her shoulder as she rushed down the hall and took another one of the side passages.

Just like any woman who wants to make certain her house is fit for company, Amelia thought as she and Daniel each took one of Nick's arms and led him in the direction Wendy had taken.

They came to a door she'd left open. The strains of White Christmas drifted toward them from inside. When they stepped across the threshold it wasn't into a bedroom. Instead it looked like a living room—in a medieval castle.

Some of the walls were stone. Others had been plastered over. Two easy chairs and a sofa were grouped around a stone fireplace where a cozy fire burned. The floors were made of wide planks, with Oriental rugs scattered around. The place seemed to represent a bunch of different styles—apparently what had struck the Clauses' fancy at any given time. And perhaps as a spur to Wendy's ideas, Amelia saw a stack of decorating magazines and catalogues on the glass-topped coffee table.

Beyond the sitting room was a short hall leading to a master bedroom with a king-sized bed made of dark heavy wood and a matching dresser and chest of drawers.

To one side was a sliding glass door, and Amelia gaped as she looked through. Instead of ice and snow, she saw a tropical scene with palm trees and a riot of flowers, a hot tub, a lap pool and a wide patio area with chaise longues and an umbrella table and chairs.

Wendy saw her staring. "Better than living in the frozen north all the time."

"Yes," Amelia managed. She tipped her head, listening to the song. "But it doesn't exactly go with White Christmas."

"It's to remind us this is just a very temporary retreat," Wendy answered.

She had already turned down the covers. Santa sat on the edge of the bed, and Wendy knelt to unlace his boots. Then he swung his legs onto the bed, and she pulled the covers over him.

"I'm not going to be here long," he muttered.

"I'm going to stay with him and make sure he gets a rest," Wendy answered.

She pulled the drapes, darkening the room, and Daniel and Amelia went back to the front of the apartment.

"Did you know about this place?" Amelia asked.

"Yes. I was here for a strategy session when I first arrived," Daniel said.

"Does the sound system always play White Christmas?"

"I don't know. I'm guessing it's a favorite, since I hear it a lot around the workshop."

"Yes." Amelia reached for his hand and folded her fingers around his palm. She thought he might pull away, but instead he shifted his hand so that his fingers were wrapped around hers. Then he slowly pulled her toward him. She came willingly, leaning her head against his shoulder as he wrapped his arms around her.

"I'd like the luxury of being with you," he said in a low voice.

"Me too," she answered. "But ..."

"I understand," she murmured.

They stood with their arms around each other, swaying slightly in the center of the room. She closed her eyes, absorbing his warmth and his masculine scent. She could have stayed there for a long time, but she knew he was right. He had work to do, and she hoped she could help him.

"I was looking for you," she said. "When Santa had his accident."

"It wasn't an accident. Someone poured that oil on the kitchen floor. And I'm betting they wanted Santa to slip and fall—not Wendy. They probably heard her asking him to take more cookies to the workshop."

"She didn't see anyone."

As she made the statement, the importance of recent events clicked into place, and she felt a jolt of excitement.

"A rat could have been in the kitchen, and she wouldn't have seen it."

"But how would a rat spill all that oil on the floor?"

"I don't know. I guess he's working with someone."

When Daniel looked doubtful, Amelia told him about her encounter with Rudolph in the barn. "He kept trying to tell me something, and I wasn't getting it. Then he showed me the clothes buried in the straw and the hole in the side of the barn."

"A rat could have dug the tunnel and gnawed the hole. But that doesn't explain the clothes."

"Let's ask Wendy."

He started back down the hall, and Amelia followed, almost bumping into him when he stopped short. Amelia looked around his shoulder and saw Wendy lying on the bed with Nick, her arms around him.

"Oh, pardon me," Daniel said, clearly embarrassed that he'd interrupted an intimate scene.

Wendy sat up. "It's all right."

Daniel cleared his throat. "I wanted to ask you a question. "Did you see any rats in the kitchen?"

Wendy's face reddened. "I was going to get Nick to take care of the problem. How did you know?"

"We're thinking the rat could be a spy," Amelia said, repeating what she'd already told Daniel.

Nick listened with interest to the exchange, then turned to his wife. "You didn't tell me anything about rats."

"I was embarrassed. I mean, I run a spotless kitchen, and I was upset about the vermin."

"They could always come over from the barn," Nick said. "It's happened before."

She gave him a chiding look. "That's not conversation for polite company."

Nick rolled his eyes.

"This could be a major breakthrough," Daniel said, then turned to Amelia. "Can you show me the hole in the barn wall?"

CHAPTER TEN

"Yes," Amelia answered.

"I'll come, too," Nick said.

Wendy's features turned firm as she put a restraining hand on his shoulder. "You will do no such thing. You will stay in bed until I say you can get up."

Nick opened his mouth, then closed it again. Apparently he'd learned over the years that there was no point in arguing with his wife when she was in full protective mode.

With a sigh, he relaxed against the pillows again.

Amelia turned away to hide a grin. Her first impression of the woman was that she let her husband make all the important decisions. Apparently, the relationship was a little more complicated.

Amelia and Daniel headed back down the hall and out of the Clauses' private quarters.

Taking the front exit, they headed for the reindeer compound. As soon as they entered, they could hear the reindeer chattering, and once again, in the middle of the din, Amelia thought she heard a foreign-sounding voice calling her name. Firmly she ignored the oddity and focused on the animals.

"Yes, we're back," she said, "And hoping Rudolph can help us." When she reached his stall, he lifted his head and started making the whining noise that she was sure could have been interpreted as reindeer distress.

"I came to show Daniel the rat hole," she said, and the clothes. Daniel got down on his hands and knees to inspect the hole. When he stood, Amelia held up the shirt and pants. "What do you make of this?"

"That either one of the workmen has been in here..."

Rudolph cut him off with a loud bellow, and Daniel looked at him inquiringly. "Not one of the workmen?"

Rudolph shook his head.

"Then who?"

The reindeer reacted as he had with Amelia.

"He wants to tell us something, but he can't speak our language."

"Too bad," Daniel answered mirroring Amelia's earlier frustration.

"Maybe it would help if we gave him more information." She turned back to Rudolph. "There was an accident in the kitchen. Santa slipped on some oil spilled on the kitchen floor."

Immediately, Rudolph and the reindeer in the other stalls began making loud noises.

"I know that's upsetting. But he's okay," Amelia said. "Mrs. Claus put him to bed. And I guess you know that any injuries he gets heal very fast."

There were murmurs of what must have been agreement from the stalls.

Amelia looked at Rudolph. "You think the rat has something to do with the sabotage?"

The reindeer nodded vigorously and began rearing up and slamming his hoofs down on the floor as though he were battering the rat to death.

Daniel sighed. "We'll try to figure it out."

Rudolph snorted.

When Daniel put a hand on Amelia's arm, she followed him out of the barn.

"What are we going to do?"

"I'd like to put up cameras in the warehouse."

"Santa said you couldn't."

"Maybe having oil spilled in his wife's kitchen will have changed his mind."

"We'll we can't ask him now."

"Right. I'm not going back into that bedroom. No telling what they're up to."

Amelia laughed, then sobered again. "When I first arrived, I could tell from your reaction that some bad things had already happened. What were they? And how many?"

"There were two incidents before I came, but Nick told me about them. The first was like the one you saw in the warehouse. Boxes fell on a workman. And there was also a fire in the corner of the back room, but that was put out very quickly. After I got here, one of the men was electrocuted by a dangling wire."

She sucked in a sharp breath. "Oh no."

"Then the avalanche. I think that was intended to take me out while I was patrolling the grounds."

"Nice." She thought for a moment. "So more problems in the warehouse than anywhere else. But others, too."

He nodded.

"Are the incidents getting closer together?" she asked.

"Yes. Nick told me they started off days apart. Now they're coming every day. As Christmas gets closer, it sounds like the culprit is more desperate to shut Santa down," Daniel mused.

"So if we were surveilling the warehouse, maybe we wouldn't have to wait too long."

"And maybe we can compromise on the setup."

"How?" Daniel added.

"Let's walk around the warehouse exterior and see if we can find the rat's secret entrance. And if we find it, we can position a camera on it."

"Good idea," Amelia agreed.

They took a stepping-stone path that went all around the main facility, their eyes trained on the bottom of the wall, looking for rat-sized holes. They found one on the side of the building that faced the barn.

Daniel went back to his office, got a small camera, and positioned it on a bracket above the hole. Then he and Amelia sat together on a love seat in the office, taking the opportunity to hold hands as they watched the camera feed. She wanted to do a lot more than that, but she knew there was too much at stake to fool around.

They had been staring at the screen for about forty minutes when both of them caught sight of movement. They sat forward as a low gray shape approached the hole. It looked like a large rat, with beady eyes and sharp teeth, and it was dragging a bag that was larger than it was."

CHAPTER ELEVEN

The creature paused and looked around, then eased through the hole in the side of the warehouse, dragging the bag after it.

"What the heck is it bringing in there?" Amelia asked. "Do you think it's a bomb?"

"I hope not."

"Well, it's slowing him down."

They sprinted to the warehouse and were in time to see the bag disappear around a shelving unit.

Daniel put a hand on her arm. "This could be dangerous. Stay back."

She shook her head. "No."

They both headed for the place where the rat had disappeared. He wasn't in sight.

"Where did he go?" Amelia whispered.

Daniel pointed to the end of the row, where the bag was just visible before disappearing around a corner.

They hurried after. But when they'd made the same turn, they both stopped dead.

The bag was open on the ground. A slender young man with messy hair, grayish skin and pointy teeth was standing beside it.

His face looked familiar, and she drew in a sharp breath. "You're the man ... who robbed my shop."

He was just tucking a long gray tail into a pair of pants—the pants Amelia had seen hidden in the straw in the barn.

She gasped, world colliding as she tried to understand what she was seeing. "What ...?"

"He's a shape-shifter," Daniel shouted, lunging at the man.

The guy looked up, alarm spreading across his face when he realized he'd been discovered. His expression turned crafty when Daniel clamped his hands over bony shoulders.

While Daniel tried to hang on to him, the man's shape started to change. Not back into the little rat they'd seen on camera but a rat that was the size of a Saint Bernard dog.

"Help," Amelia shouted. "It's the saboteur. Don't let him get away."

Men from the warehouse came running, but when they saw that the menace was a huge rat with sharp claws and long teeth, they backed off, and she didn't blame them.

Those teeth clacked as it rose up on its hind legs, lunging for Daniel.

Amelia threw herself down, grabbed for it's tail and held on. It turned on her, teeth snapping, but Daniel had pulled a box that said "unicycles" from the shelves.

He pulled out one of the machines and brought it down on the rat's head. The beast must have had tremendous stamina, because the blow didn't stop it. It turned and lunged for Amelia again. When she screamed and dropped the tail, the rat galloped toward the main entrance.

But before it reached safety, Nick strode into the doorway, looking as fit as before he'd taken the fall in the kitchen. His eyes flashed with anger as he confronted the source of all their recent troubles.

"It's a shape-shifter," Daniel shouted. "It came in as a small rat, then turned into a man. And now this."

The beast stopped short, looking behind itself at the crowd of people. Then it turned toward the door again, probably figuring that it had a better chance with one old man who'd already taken a bad fall.

But when the rat dodged right, Nick was in front of him in a flash. And when it went left, Nick countered the move.

The shifter snarled. To Amelia's astonishment, it shouted words. "Out of my way, you old fairy tale."

"And what are you, a demon?"

"What if I am?"

"Go back and tell your master you failed."

The rat howled, his voice sounding part defiant and part frightened.

While Nick blocked the animal's escape, Daniel was rummaging through more boxes.

This time he found the parts for a swing set. Among them were long metal poles. Daniel snatched one up and used it as a lance. Amelia looked away as he ran the animal through, and it lay twitching on the floor.

She stared at it in horror, still trying to absorb what had happened.

"I've never seen a shape-shifter before," she whispered. "I didn't even know they were real."

Santa nodded. "As real as any other mythical creature. They're not all bad. Some fight for the good and true. But when they are evil, they're rotten to the core." He looked at Daniel. "Good work. Now we don't have to worry about all those children not getting their toys."

"Yes. But I couldn't have done it without Amelia. You were right. We needed an outsider to see things we couldn't."

"I'm just glad I could help," she murmured as she raised questioning eyes to Daniel.

She expected to see a look of satisfaction on his face. Instead, he looked sad.

"What?"

"I think my work here is done."

Amelia heard a note of finality in his voice. "What do you mean?"

"I have to go."

"No." Ignoring the crowd of watchers in the room, she rushed toward him clasping her arms around his shoulders. He pulled her closer, his lips coming down on hers for a long bittersweet kiss. And then, like the man who had gotten injured at the beginning, she felt Daniel become less solid.

Did she hear him whisper? "Maybe I can..."

The tone of his voice gave a little jolt of hope. "Maybe you can what?"

Daniel didn't answer. And when she opened her eyes, her heart turned over. She saw his body fading away.

"No. Please no."

And when she looked at her own hand, she saw she was doing the same thing.

She tried to clutch onto Daniel at the same time she willed her own body to stay solid. But hanging on to Santaland seemed impossible.

The scene faded around her. Dimly she saw Nick and Wendy and the workmen ranged around her.

And then she was nowhere. In endless blackness. It was like when she'd first been hit by the car.

CHAPTER TWELVE

Amelia heard someone cry out. This time she knew it was her.

Then someone was calling her name, and she prayed it was Daniel—that he was with her. But she couldn't convince herself it was him. It was the man with a foreign-sounding accent whom she'd heard before— when she was with the reindeer. Now his voice was coming through more clearly.

"Amelia." he said. "Open your eyes and look at me, Amelia."

She didn't want to do it. She wanted to stay where she was and hope that she could get back to Santaland, but the man kept talking to her. "I am Dr. Singh. You were in an accident, and you've been in a coma."

That got her attention. In a coma?

Her lids fluttered open, and she found herself staring into warm brown eyes.

"You're awake."

She licked dry lips, still struggling with a feeling of deep loss.

She was in one of those hospital beds with railings at the sides. And the bed was surrounded by monitoring equipment. When she tried to push herself up, he put a hand on her shoulder. "You must take it easy."

"What happened?"

"You were hit by a car. The police think it was the man who robbed your shop. They have him in custody."

She tried to take that in as a nurse bustled about, using a stylus to write on a tablet.

"An FBI agent has been here, anxious for you to wake up."

"Yes. I remember someone called me."

"I told him he'd have to wait until you're better, but he says it's urgent. The police can't hold the man on just a hit and run charge."

She felt utterly confused, utterly worn out just with the effort to talk. "I can't see anyone now."

"I understand," the doctor said. "I'll explain your condition to him."

One wall of the room was made of glass, and she could see a man pacing back and forth in the hall.

When she caught a glimpse of his face, her heart lurched.

"No, wait. Tell him to come in."

The doctor went to the door and motioned to the man. Amelia could see he was tall with broad shoulders and intense eyes.

Beside her, the nurse pressed a button to raise the back of the bed.

"Amelia," the man said as he came toward her bed.

"Daniel?"

He looked surprised. "You remember me from that phone call a couple of days ago? I thought you could barely understand who I was and what I wanted."

"Yes, but ... Nick told me your name."

"Nick who?"

She closed her eyes for a moment, thinking that if she tried to explain, she was going to sound crazy and they'd transfer right to the psychiatric ward.

Instead, she whispered, "Who are you?"

"Special Agent Daniel Blake. FBI."

"Okay."

He leaned closer, "I'm sorry to press you when you've just woken up, but we have a situation here. When your shop was robbed, it looked like one of the ordinary robberies in the area, but we think it's connected with a drug smuggling operation."

"Drug smuggling? How?"

"Drugs were hidden in some of the items you imported."

She made a strangled sound. "You're sure? I mean, how could that be?"

"We know you're not involved in the smuggling. The shipment was sent to you by mistake. But I need you to look at some pictures and tell me if one of them is the man who robbed your shop. I know it's been several months, but I'm hoping you can pick him out."

"Okay," she said again.

The nurse stepped to her side, searching her face. "You've just been through a medical crisis. You're sure you're up to this?"

"Yes."

Daniel pulled up a chair, sat down, and showed her the pictures one at a time. When he came to the fourth one, she made a strangled sound. It was the man who had changed into a huge rat. And it was also the same man who had knocked her to the ground when he was dashing out the back door of her shop.

"Him," she said.

"You're sure."

"Very sure. It's like I saw him a couple of hours ago."

"Okay good. That's very helpful."

He stood and hurried from the room, and she closed her eyes again, drifting off. As she slept, she felt people standing on either side of the bed. She didn't open her eyes, but she knew it was Nick and Wendy and some of the men from the workshop.

She turned to where she was sure Nick stood. "You knew, didn't you?"

He made a noncommital sound, but Wendy said, "We liked knowing you were going to be happy."

"Why couldn't you tell me?"

"We never reveal the future."

Maybe it was hours later when she opened her eyes again. Daniel was sitting in the armchair in the corner of the room, reading a book. She blinked when she saw a tin of cookies on the small table beside him. It was a lot like one of the tins that had been in Wendy's kitchen.

"Cookies?" she asked in a weak voice.

"Your friend, Melinda, brought them."

"Oh," she answered, then added, "She does like to bake."

He smiled at her, got up, and took the small chair near the bed. She smiled back.

"A lot of your friends came in to see you."

For a moment she was confused. Did he know about Nick and Wendy?

"Women from town. There are flowers from the group." He gestured toward a vase on the chest by the door.

"Oh, my friends. Right. I'm sorry I missed them."

"They said they'd see you at home. I think they're organizing to bring you dinner for a week or so. And Melinda said not to worry about the hospital tree. They've got it covered."

She was overwhelmed by all the thoughtfulness. "That's so nice."

"How are you feeling?"

"Better."

"Good. We were all worried about you."

"I'm almost back to normal. Can you crank up my bed?"

"Sure." He pressed the button that raised the headrest, then sat again.

"I got to know you while you were in a coma," he said.

Startled, she asked, "How?"

She'd certainly gotten to know him, but she was pretty sure he hadn't shared the experience.

"I read those newspaper articles about you. Then I found the videos you'd made for the St. Stephens Business Association—the ones showing visitors around the area."

"Right. I got to play hometown tour guide."

It was hard not to add, "And I got to know you while I was asleep," but she stopped herself because she didn't want to come across as a nut case.

"Dr. Singh told me you can go home tomorrow."

"That's good news." She played with the edge of the sheet. "I guess I'll have to start calling some of those friends to find a ride home."

"I can do it," he said, and she saw him flush slightly.

"Don't you have work to do?"

"Yeah, but my time is flexible."

He looked at her hand, and she was sure for a moment that he would reach for it. But he kept his own hands clasped in his lap. She wondered what he was feeling—or how much he was feeling.

It seemed insane to think that they'd made a connection while she was unconscious. But at the same time, she was sure it was true. Even if some of the details were different, his character was so much like the man she remembered—once he'd been able to trust her.

He looked like he wanted to say more. She certainly did. But she understood there would be time. And maybe when she got closer to him, she'd explain about their saving Santaland.

She knew a grin was flickering on her lips.

"What?"

"I had a really interesting dream while I was out of it," She said.

And for now that was all she was going to reveal.

THE END

If you enjoyed WHITE CHRISTMAS, you might also like to read other Light Street Press books by Rebecca York:

DECORAH SECURITY SERIES
(sexy paranormal romantic suspense)
BY REBECCA YORK

#1. ON EDGE (e-book novella and Decorah prequel).

#2. DARK MOON (e-book and trade paperback novel).

#3. CHAINED (e-book novella).

#4. AMBUSHED (e-book short story).

#5. DARK POWERS (e-book and trade paperback novel).

#6. HOT AND DANGEROUS (e-book short story).

#7. AT RISK (e-book and trade paperback novel).

#8. CHRISTMAS CAPTIVE (e-book novella).

#9. DESTINATION WEDDING (e-book novella).

#10. RX MISSING (e-book and trade paperback novel)

#11. HUNTING MOON (a novel)

#12. TERROR MENSION (a novella)

#13. OUTLAW JUSTICE (a novella)

#14. FOUND MISSING (a novel)

DECORAH SECURITY COLLECTION (e-book including *Ambushed, Hot and Dangerous, Chained,* and *Dark Powers*).

OFF-WORLD SERIES
(sexy science-fiction romance)
BY REBECCA YORK

#1. HERO'S WELCOME (e-book romance short story).

#2. NIGHTFALL (e-book romance novella).

#3. CONQUEST (e-book romance short story).

#4. ASSIGNMENT DANGER (e-book romance novella).

#5. CHRISTMAS HOME (e-book romance short story).

#6. FIRELIGHT CONFESSION (e-book romance novella)

OFF WORLD COLLECTION (e-book including *Nightfall, Hero's Welcome,* and *Conquest*).

PRAISE FOR REBECCA YORK

Rebecca York delivers page-turning suspense.
—Nora Roberts

Rebecca York never fails to deliver. Her strong characterizations, imaginative plots and sensuous love scenes have made fans of thousands of romance, romantic suspense and thriller readers.
—Chassie West

Rebecca York will thrill you with romance, kill you with danger and chill you with the supernatural.
—Patricia Rosemoor

(Rebecca York) is a real luminary of contemporary series romance
—Michael Dirda, The Washington Post Book World

Rebecca York's writing is fast-paced, suspenseful, and loaded with tension.
—Jayne Ann Krentz

ABOUT THE AUTHOR

A New York Times and USA Today Best-Selling Author, Rebecca York is a 2011 recipient of the Romance Writers of America Centennial Award. Her career has focused on romantic suspense, often with paranormal elements.

Her 16 Berkley books and novellas include her nine-book werewolf "Moon" series. KILLING MOON was a launch book for the Berkley Sensation imprint. She has written for Harlequin, Berkley, Dell, Tor, Carina Press, Silhouette, Kensington, Running Press, Tudor, Pageant Books, and Scholastic.

Her many awards include two Rita finalist books. She has two Career Achievement awards from Romantic Times: for Series Romantic Suspense and for Series Romantic Mystery. And her Peregrine Connection series won a Lifetime Achievement Award for Romantic Suspense Series.

Many of her novels have been nominated for or won RT Reviewers Choice awards. In addition, she has won a Prism Award, several New Jersey Romance Writers Golden Leaf awards and numerous other awards.

Web site: www.RebeccaYork.com
E-mail: rebecca@rebeccayork.com
Facebook: www.facebook.com/ruthglick
Twitter: @rebeccayork43
Blog: www.rebeccayork.blogspot.com

www.ingramcontent.com/pod-product-compliance
Lightning Source LLC
Chambersburg PA
CBHW070534130626
46555CB00003B/1414